Mystery at the BILTMORE

The Classified Catnapping

by COLLEEN NELSON

illustrated by PEGGY COLLINS

First published in Canada and the United States in 2025

Text copyright © 2025 Colleen Nelson
Illustration copyright © 2025 Peggy Collins
This edition copyright © 2025 Pajama Press Inc.
This is a first edition

10 9 8 7 6 5 4 3 2 1

All rights reserved. No part of this publication may be reproduced, stored in a retrieval system or transmitted, in any form or by any means, without the prior written consent of the publisher or a licence from The Canadian Copyright Licensing Agency (Access Copyright). For an Access Copyright licence, visit www.accesscopyright.ca or call toll free 1.800.893.5777.
www.pajamapress.ca   info@pajamapress.ca

 Canada Council   Conseil des arts
for the Arts   du Canada

 Ontario
 Canadä

The publisher gratefully acknowledges the support of the Canada Council for the Arts and the Ontario Arts Council for its publishing program. We acknowledge the financial support of the Government of Canada through the Canada Book Fund (CBF) for our publishing activities.

Library and Archives Canada Cataloguing in Publication

Title: The classified catnapping / by Colleen Nelson ; illustrated by Peggy Collins.
Names: Nelson, Colleen, author. | Collins, Peggy, 1975- illustrator.
Description: First edition. | Series statement: Mystery at the Biltmore ; 2
Identifiers: Canadiana 20240485505 | ISBN 9781772783360 (hardcover)
Subjects: LCGFT: Detective and mystery fiction. | LCGFT: Novels.
Classification: LCC PS8627.E555 C53 2025 | DDC jC813/.6—dc23

Publisher Cataloging-in-Publication Data (U.S.)

Names: Nelson, Colleen, author | Collins, Peggy, 1975-, illustrator.
Title: Mystery at the Biltmore 2 : the classified catnapping / by Colleen Nelson ; illustrated by Peggy Collins.
Description: First edition. | Toronto, Ontario : Pajama Press ; La Vergne, TN :
   Distributed in the U.S. by Publishers Group West, 2025. | Series: Mystery at the
   Biltmore, 2. | Summary: "The LaRue Detective Agency has gained a reputation at
   The Biltmore as the investigators to call, so it's no surprise when Elodie is asked to
   solve a top-secret catnapping case, which she tackles undercover as a journalist"—
   Provided by publisher.
Identifiers: ISBN 978-1-77278-336-0 (hardcover)
Subjects: LCSH: Detectives–Juvenile fiction. | Cats–Juvenile fiction. | Lost and found possessions–Juvenile fiction. | Apartment houses–New York (State)–New York–Juvenile fiction. | New York (N.Y.)–Juvenile fiction. | BISAC: JUVENILE FICTION / Mysteries & Detective Stories. | JUVENILE FICTION / Girls & Women. | JUVENILE FICTION / Social Themes / Friendship. | JUVENILE FICTION / Law & Crime. | JUVENILE FICTION / Lifestyles / City & Town Life. | JUVENILE FICTION / Places / United States.
Classification: LCC PZ7. N424 Mys 2025 | DDC [Fic] – dc23

Cover and interior art—Peggy Collins
Cover and book design—Simin Dewji

Printed in China

This book was designed with left alignment and generous spacing to improve the reading experience for readers of all neurotypes.

Pajama Press Inc.
11 Davies Avenue, Suite 103, Toronto, Ontario Canada, M4M 2A9

Distributed in Canada by UTP Distribution | 5201 Dufferin Street Toronto, Ontario Canada, M3H 5T8
Distributed in the U.S. by Publishers Group West | 1 Ingram Blvd. La Vergne, TN 37086, USA

For Cindy Kochanski
—C.N.

For Soila and Nema ♥
—P.C.

Chapter 1
ELODIE

There were many mysteries at The Biltmore, a hundred-year-old building in New York City's Upper West Side, but there had never been a murder. Until today.

It happened in the courtyard, in plain view of all the residents, including Elodie LaRue and Oscar Delgado who watched from up in #5D.

The victim lay on the red brick path…and he wasn't alone. From her perch on the edge of the fountain, a fluffy cat with fur the color of buttercream icing, leapt to the ground. She walked around the body, flicked her tail, and disappeared under a boxwood hedge. The only evidence of her presence was a trail of bloody paw prints.

"Cut!" The director's voice rang out, startling Elodie and Oscar. The children had been glued to the window for hours, watching the action below. It was a welcome distraction for Elodie. Her parents, international art crime investigators, had dashed off earlier that week in hot pursuit of another thief.

She wished they could have stayed to see the courtyard transformed into a movie set. There were trailers set up for the actors, cameras on cranes, and a row of director's chairs with names painted on the back. Some of the apartments at The Biltmore had been used as sets for movies before—lots of writers and actors lived in the building—but never the courtyard. It was the first time the residents had a bird's eye view of a film production.

Miss Rosa, Elodie's nanny, placed a tray of juice and muffins on the table between their chairs. The scent of fresh baking and the promise of a few crumbs roused Elodie's dog, a West Highland Terrier named Carnegie, from her nap. Elodie moved over and patted the space beside her. Carnegie jumped up, turned around, and wiggled her bottom until she was comfortable, then lay down.

Shooting a movie was a slow process, but Elodie and Oscar didn't want to miss a moment. "Look! There he is!" Oscar pointed excitedly as the man with the knife sticking out of his back stood up.

Most people fawned over the lead actor, but not Oscar. It was the lead actor's stunt double, Lance Beauregard, that had his attention. Oscar's dream was to one day be doing the same thing as his idol. It wasn't far-fetched either. Oscar could parkour and ride a unicycle better than anyone Elodie had ever met.

Down below, Freddy, the building's doorman waved at the kids as two make-up people dabbed powder on his forehead.

He'd been cast in the movie as an extra but had to trade in his usual dapper uniform for something more traditional. The stiff suit with the gold braid didn't match Freddy's personality at all.

"Quiet on set!" a production assistant shouted. Elodie leaned closer to the window. The hubbub below died down. "Action!"

Elodie gave Carnegie a pat. With Oscar on one side, her dog on the other, and Miss Rosa reading nearby, Elodie was quite content. So content, thoughts of her parents and the mysteries they were solving faded to the back of her mind. With good friends and her own detective agency to keep her busy, Elodie was having a most enjoyable summer holiday. And the good news was: it was just getting started.

Chapter 2
TIYA

The trailers, cameras, and director's chairs were still in the courtyard the next day, but the set was quiet. Yesterday's shoot had gone late into the night, so the crew had the day off. Elodie knew that some of the residents would be relieved at the break. Not everyone had been in favor of turning their home into a movie set.

Oscar interrupted Elodie's thoughts as he placed three cups in front of her. Under the middle cup was a small blue ball. "You need to guess where the ball is," he told her, then began switching the positions of the cups. Elodie kept her eyes on the cup he had placed the ball under but knew there was probably more to this trick than she expected. For the last few days, Oscar had been practicing magic tricks. It was one more skill he could add to his stunt person repertoire.

Oscar finished shifting the cups with a flourish of his hands and stood back. "Where's the ball?"

Elodie looked at the three identical cups. Logic told her the ball was under the middle one, but Oscar's tricks had been improving. Should she guess a different cup? "That one," she said, pointing to the cup on the right.

Oscar grinned and lifted it. Nothing was there. He lifted the one on the left. No ball. "I knew I should have picked the middle one," Elodie said. But, when Oscar picked up that cup, the ball wasn't there either. Elodie looked at her friend, mystified. Since Oscar had moved in at the beginning of the summer holidays, things at The Biltmore had become far more interesting. "How'd you do that?"

Oscar couldn't resist telling her. "It's called the French Drop. While you were distracted looking at the cups, I snuck the ball into my sleeve." Elodie *had* thought it was odd that Oscar was wearing a long-sleeved shirt on a hot summer day. She shook her head at the missed clue. As the lead investigator of the LaRue Detective Agency, she should have put two and two together. Or not. What was the fun of magic if she knew all the answers?

"It was a very good trick," she complimented Oscar. "I wonder if Carnegie would fall for it." With Carnegie's excellent sense of smell and naturally inquisitive nature, it was hard to pull a fast one on her. At the mention of her name, Carnegie bounded over.

Oscar put a treat, instead of a ball, under one of the cups and switched their places, just as he'd done for Elodie. Carnegie sat watching intently. Her black nose wiggled. "Where's the treat, Carnegie?"

Unlike Elodie, Carnegie got it right on the first try.

Their laughter was interrupted by a knock at the door. A girl, about ten-years-old with dark, curly hair and brown eyes stood in the hall. While the movie had been filming, Elodie had seen this girl in the courtyard. Her name was Tiya Benson, and she wasn't a resident, not usually anyway. She was visiting her mother, Paula, who lived on the tenth floor.

The smiling, bright-eyed girl Elodie had seen in the courtyard looked nothing like the worried, jittery one in front of her now. "Are you Elodie LaRue? The detective?" Tiya asked.

Hearing those words sent a shiver of excitement up Elodie's spine. With Oscar and Carnegie's help, the LaRue Detective Agency had gained a reputation at The Biltmore as *the* investigators to call.

"Yes. What can we do to help?" Elodie reached for the notebook she kept by the door for just these situations.

Tiya glanced up and down the hall. "May I come in?"

"Of course." Elodie stepped aside. Her sharp detective eye missed nothing. The fingernails on both of Tiya's hands were short and ragged. *She's been chewing them*, Elodie realized. *She's worried about something*.

Carnegie raced over, eager to greet the new visitor. Tiya stepped back, startled. "Does he bite?"

"She," Elodie corrected. "And no. Or, at least, she never has." Although Elodie couldn't imagine Carnegie biting anyone.

"I'm scared of dogs," the girl admitted, eyeing Carnegie and edging into the apartment.

"You're more of a cat person," Elodie guessed, noting the long, pale strands of cat hair stuck to Tiya's clothing.

Tiya gave a weak smile. "I guess you could say that."

Oscar shut the door and Elodie led the way to her office, which was really a large pantry off the kitchen. Miss Rosa had removed the shelves and spruced it up with wallpaper and an ornate light fixture. She'd also painted a sign on the door that read 'LaRue Detective Agency.' With enough room for three chairs, a dog bed for Carnegie, and a fold-out desk for Elodie, it was private and perfect for taking meetings.

Tiya waited until the door was closed before she said, "I need your help." There was no mistaking the desperation in her voice. "I have a really big problem."

"Start at the beginning," Elodie said, straightening the bow in her hair and smoothing her skirt. Elodie thought it important to always look professional. She didn't mind Oscar's more casual style of shorts and a t-shirt, but, for her, a well-coordinated outfit showed her attention to detail, an important quality for a detective.

"Do you know Bijou? The cat?" Elodie and Oscar nodded. Of course, they knew Bijou! She was the star of the movie. "And you probably knew her owner."

"The fashion designer Lucien Saint Martin," Elodie answered. A remarkable talent in the design world, Lucien had passed away suddenly last year. While his death had come as a surprise, it was what he did with his fortune that was the real shocker.

His apartment at The Biltmore and his entire fortune had not been left to his family or friends, but to Bijou! Overnight, she became the world's wealthiest feline.

"My mom is Bijou's nanny. When Monsieur Saint Martin died, she moved into his apartment to look after Bijou full-time. I'm staying with her for the rest of summer vacation." Tiya leaned in and dropped her voice. "What I have to tell you is a secret. *No one* can know."

"You can trust us," Oscar said.

Elodie nodded. Discretion, knowing what to say and when to say it, was an important part of being a detective.

"This morning, before my mom left, we had an argument in the elevator."

"About what?" Elodie asked.

"What we always argue about." Tiya rolled her eyes. "Bijou and why Mom had to move *here* to take care of a cat. Why can't Bijou move to Queens? I mean, she's a cat, not royalty. Does it really matter where she lives? But every time I bring it up, Mom shuts me down. She says living here is what Monsieur Saint Martin wanted for Bijou, and as the nanny she has to honor his wishes. She cares more about keeping the cat happy than me." Tiya frowned. Clearly, the memory of the argument was still fresh.

"And?" Elodie prompted.

"And…as we were getting off the elevator, I said…" Tiya paused, wincing. "I wished Bijou would disappear. And now she has! Bijou is missing."

"Missing?" Oscar repeated. "Like she escaped? Ran away?" Many of the residents at The Biltmore had pets. Oscar, Elodie, and Carnegie had tracked down a few of them since the LaRue Detective Agency had opened.

Tiya shook her head. "No, she was stolen! And if I can't find her my mom is going to lose her job. You have to help me!"

Elodie sat up straighter in her chair. This certainly sounded like it had the makings of a case. "Tell us everything you know about Bijou's disappearance."

"Don't leave anything out," Oscar cautioned.

Tiya pulled herself together. "You know Spaw, the pet grooming place on 83rd St.?" Spaw was the poshest place to pamper your pet. It had separate entrances for cats and dogs. Carnegie didn't go there, but many pets of The Biltmore residents did. "Mom dropped Bijou off this morning. But she had all this running around to do for tonight's party and couldn't pick Bijou up, so she asked me to. She arranged for a car and everything. I was supposed to get there at ten o'clock, but I was late."

"Traffic?" Oscar asked.

Tiya shook her head. "Museum of Natural History."

Elodie paused in her note-taking, confused. What did the museum have to do with being late to pick up Bijou from Spaw? "I've been here for five days already and every time I ask Mom to do *anything* she says no. First, it was because Bijou was in the movie, and today it was errands. I thought since I had a driver…"

"You'd do some sightseeing on your own," Elodie finished.

"Yeah, but without Mom, it wasn't very fun. I left halfway through the African Mammals Gallery. By the time I got to Spaw, Bijou was gone."

Elodie and Oscar exchanged a look. "She was taken from Spaw?"

Tiya nodded. "When I arrived, I said I was there to pick up Bijou. The woman at the front desk looked confused. She said Bijou had already been picked up. Someone had called about fifteen minutes earlier, asking for Bijou to be brought out to a car waiting at the curb. A lot of famous people do that, so she didn't think anything of it. She put Bijou in her cat carrier and handed her to the driver who placed her in the backseat. The receptionist never saw the passenger and couldn't even tell me if it was a man or a woman."

Elodie tapped her pen on her notebook and exchanged a look with Oscar. She turned to Tiya. "I'll need to call Spaw for more details. Maybe the receptionist remembers a clue about the person who called. I'll speak to your mom too, since she is the full-time nanny."

Tiya shook her head. "You can't!"

"Why not? They will have valuable information."

"Because I don't want my mom to know.

I told you about our argument. It'll be bad enough admitting I went to the museum by myself. But if she finds out that it's my fault Bijou is missing, she'll be so mad. Sometimes it feels—" Tiya broke off, collected herself, and tried again, but this time her voice was barely a whisper. "Like she cares more about Bijou than me."

"I'm sure that's not true," Elodie said, gently. "Don't you think you should tell her the truth?"

"No," Tiya shook her head, adamant. "That's why I'm here. I won't have to tell her anything if you find Bijou before the party tonight."

Elodie frowned, closing her notebook. She didn't agree with Tiya's decision to keep things a secret. Part of her wondered if she should refuse to take the case. But then she glanced at Carnegie, snoring peacefully on her bed.

Bijou might have been a catrillionaire, but she was also a pet. Elodie opened her notebook and asked Tiya to go over the morning's events one more time. She resolved, with Oscar and Carnegie's help, that she would crack this catnapping case and bring Bijou home.

Chapter 3

MRS. FINEMAN

Keeping the case classified, and not revealing that Bijou was missing would make the investigation tricky, but Elodie was unfazed. "You mentioned a party," Elodie said, referring to her notes. "What kind?"

"A birthday party for Bijou. She's turning eight. All Monsieur Saint Martin's friends are invited, the people from the movie—"

"*All* the movie people?" Oscar asked, suddenly interested. His mom had warned him not to make a nuisance of himself by hanging around the set, but he was desperate to meet Lance.

Tiya nodded and kept listing off the guests. "Bijou's official photographer, of course; her biographer; and Monsieur Saint Martin's family, not that they'll come."

Elodie jotted this information down and turned the conversation back to the missing cat. "What did you do when you realized Bijou wasn't at Spaw?"

"I pretended like it was fine but inside I was having a meltdown! I told the driver Bijou wasn't ready yet and Mom would pick her up later. He dropped me back off here and I came to find you."

"You were smart to act fast. The first 24 hours of any case are crucial for finding evidence." Elodie turned to Oscar. "We'll start with some fieldwork."

Fieldwork meant interviewing possible suspects, surveying the crime scene, and looking for clues. But since Elodie wasn't allowed to leave The Biltmore and Tiya had sworn her to secrecy, all the fieldwork would have to be done discreetly and within the building. *This might be our toughest case yet,* Elodie thought to herself as she tied a bow around Carnegie's neck, a signal that it was time to get to work.

Oscar leapt into action too. "Don't worry, Tiya. You've come to the right place. The LaRue Detective Agency will find that feline."

Up until now, Oscar had restrained himself from his usual antics. Once they were waiting for the elevator, he let loose. There was nothing more tempting for a future stuntperson than a long, quiet stretch of apartment corridor to practice a tumbling routine. Elodie was used to his demonstrations and reread the notes she'd taken, but Tiya stared open-mouthed. "You're like that stuntman in the movie!"

"Lance Beauregard?" Oscar snorted. "No way. That guy's a legend! I'd love to meet him."

Tiya wrinkled her nose. "I didn't like him much. He kept complaining to Alfie about Bijou. First, that he was allergic to her and then that it was unfair Bijou got a chair with her name on it and he didn't."

"Who's Alfie?" Elodie asked.

"Bijou's agent. Lance's too." Elodie made a note of it. Detectives never knew what information would prove useful.

She closed her investigation diary and tightened her grip on Carnegie's leash. She could hear a commotion in the elevator and knew they were in for a bumpy ride.

Many types of animals lived at The Biltmore, but like people, they weren't all easy to get along with. As the elevator drew closer, agitated barks and growls could be heard, and Carnegie's tail went up. "Maybe we should take the stairs," Oscar suggested. "Or wait for another elevator?"

But it was too late. The doors had opened.

Mrs. Fineman held onto her freshly groomed, and very noisy, Pomeranian, Lawrence. His white hair stood out like a lion's mane on his tiny frame. Lawrence and Mrs. Fineman were both known in the building for their bite. Mr. Franklin and his Great Dane, Rupert, were still as statues, trying to ignore the yapping dog. Mr. Franklin gave Elodie a helpless look as she, Oscar, Tiya, and Carnegie stepped in.

Rupert bowed his head to greet Carnegie nose to nose. The two dogs were good friends. "Hello, Elodie," Mr. Franklin said with a nod. "Oscar."

There was no point introducing Tiya, since Elodie's voice would be drowned out by the racket Lawrence was making. Mrs. Fineman reached into her purse and offered Lawrence a treat. The strong smell of fish filled the air. Mr. Franklin covered his nose discreetly, but Oscar couldn't help himself. "That stinks! What is that?"

"Freeze-dried herring," Mrs. Fineman said. "My Lawrence loves it." It was true. Lawrence fell silent as he gobbled up the treats, but the second they were gone, the barking resumed.

Finally, they reached Mr. Franklin's floor and Elodie gave a sigh of relief. Mr. Franklin was about to step out of the elevator when he dug into his jacket pocket and pulled out a business card. "I've been meaning to give this to you," he said, passing the card to Mrs. Fineman.

She read it as the doors closed and let out a huff of disgust. "An animal trainer!" she exclaimed. "Is Mr. Franklin suggesting that's what I need for Lawrence?"

Elodie had been living in The Biltmore long enough to know that it was best not to engage with Mrs. Fineman. She shot Oscar a look, reminding him of the same. As the editor of *The Biltmore Bulletin*, Mrs. Fineman wrote about the goings-on of the building. Sometimes she stirred up controversy with her strong opinions. She was one of the people who didn't think the courtyard should be used to film a movie. "Our beloved Biltmore is a home, not a Hollywood set," she'd written in last month's Letter from the Editor. It had caused quite a stir when it came out.

Elodie wondered if it wasn't the film that was the problem, but its star. She'd heard rumors that Mrs. Fineman had raised a ruckus when she found out that Bijou was to inherit Monsieur Saint Martin's apartment, calling it "disgraceful."

"Will the cat come to our annual meetings? Shall we serve kibble hors d'oeuvres at the next party?" she'd ask anyone who'd listen. "Lucien Saint Martin has turned The Biltmore into the laughingstock of the Upper West Side!"

Mrs. Fineman drew herself to her full height, indignant. "My Lawrence is not poorly behaved. Look how he is with your Carnegie. An angel. It's that dog of Mr. Franklin's. He's just too large for our building. He intimidates my Lawrence."

The elevator arrived on Mrs. Fineman's floor. She and Lawrence exited without a backward glance. The smell of freeze-dried herring went with her, but not the business card from Mr. Franklin. Before it hit the ground, Oscar scooped it up, and made it disappear with a flourish. Tiya's eyes widened. "Where'd it go?"

"Hmm? I think I saw it over here," Oscar said and, to Tiya's delight, made the card reappear from behind her ear. Elodie had to admit, Oscar's sleight of hand was improving. With a bow, he passed the card to Elodie so she could read it.

There was a photo of Ramon with a cat draped around his shoulders and a dog on his lap. Elodie remembered seeing Ramon on set when Bijou had been filming in the courtyard. Was he a person of interest? Elodie wasn't sure, so, for now, she tucked the business card into her investigation diary.

Chapter 4
PAULA

Finally, the elevator arrived on the tenth floor. As if knowing her services were needed, Carnegie led the way to Bijou's apartment. Bred as ratters, West Highland Terriers were known for their excellent sense of smell and tenacious nature. Two qualities that were helpful in detective work.

"How are you going to ask Paula questions about Bijou without telling her the cat is missing?" Oscar whispered to Elodie. Elodie had been mulling over this problem as well. It was the chance meeting with Mrs. Fineman that had given her an idea.

"I'm going undercover."

An undercover operation was a ruse, or an act, detectives used to get information they wanted. Her parents often posed as wealthy art buyers to arrange clandestine meetings with suspected art thieves. For this case, Elodie was going to pretend to be the newest reporter for *The Biltmore Bulletin*.

Tiya opened the door to the apartment. A large three-bedroom, it was decorated in elegant creams and grays. There was a gourmet kitchen, hardwood floors, and art that would have made Miss Rosa swoon. This had been Monsieur Saint Martin's main residence, and it swam with his good taste, but here and there, Paula and Tiya's lives had crept in. The book Tiya must have been reading was open on the coffee table. The toe of a running shoe peeked out of the not-quite-closed closet door and the fridge was cluttered with notes and notices, including a list of important phone numbers.

Modern Cat and *Cat World* magazine covers featuring Bijou were framed and hanging on the wall. All over the apartment were photos of Bijou and Monsieur Saint Martin in Paris, Venice, and Rio de Janeiro. Bijou had traveled all over the world with the designer before his untimely death.

Oscar juggled some cat toys. "I bet these toys are covered in Bijou's scent." One by one, he tossed them in Carnegie's direction; although, as Carnegie raced after them, it looked like the two of them were having more fun than finding clues.

Elodie turned to Tiya. It was time to move on to the next part of her plan.

Questioning people was like peeking under Oscar's magic cups. Sometimes she came up empty, but other times, if she paid attention, a prize was revealed. What would she find when she dug into this case?

Tiya picked up the receiver on an antique-looking phone and dialed her mom's number.

Paula answered right away and the two exchanged some typical mother-daughter pleasantries. There was no hint of the earlier argument. "Someone from *The Biltmore Bulletin* is doing a story on Bijou. She's here right now and wants to ask you some questions." Tiya nodded, listening to her mom's reply, then passed the phone to Elodie. "She says she'd be happy to, but she doesn't have much time. Also, the article can't be published until Alfie approves it."

Elodie agreed, then took the phone and introduced herself.

On the other end of the phone, Paula let out a surprised laugh. "Oh, you're a child! I was expecting someone older! What would you like to know?" It wasn't the first time an interview subject had been disarmed by Elodie's age. While being a young detective could sometimes work against her, she'd discovered that people were often willing to share things they wouldn't with an adult.

"Oh, everything!" Elodie gushed, 'in character' as an avid Bijou fan. "What's Bijou's personality like?"

Paula laughed. "She's a diva! Monsieur Saint Martin spoiled her rotten! He used to say, 'Only the best for Mademoiselle!' And he meant it! He hired personal chefs to prepare her food and only bought her the best seafood. Once she got a taste for gambas rojas de Dénia, that was it. She refused to touch another bowl of kibble."

"What are *gambas rojas de Dénia*?" Elodie asked, hoping she'd spelled it correctly in her investigation diary.

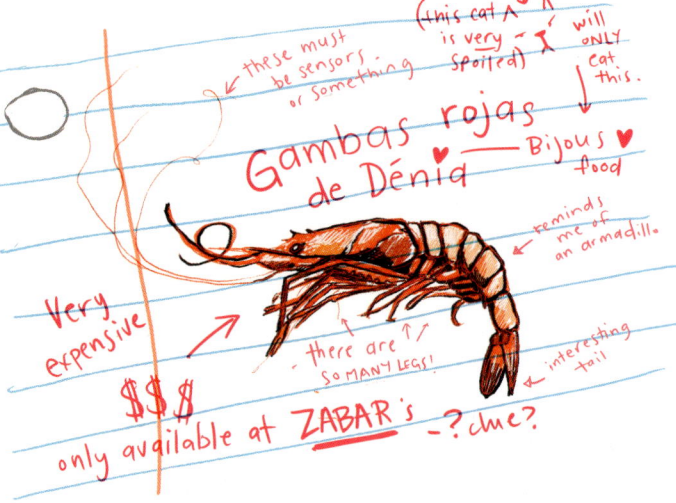

"The world's most expensive shrimp. Zabar's flies them in just for Bijou." Zabar's was the legendary Upper West Side deli and grocery store frequented by The Biltmore's residents. "I've tried feeding her other foods, but she starts meowing in protest until I give her the shrimp. Like I said, she's spoiled."

"But not too spoiled to work? I saw her on set in the courtyard."

Paula's voice changed. It went from warm and open to guarded. "I don't have anything to do with her career, that's all Alfie. Honestly, Bijou would probably prefer to be curled up in her cat condo or cuddling on the couch." Paula's voice softened. She clearly cared for Bijou, despite the cat's diva behavior.

"Do you like your job? What's it like caring for the world's wealthiest cat?" This question had nothing to do with Bijou and everything to do with the investigation. Thankfully, Paula didn't notice.

"I do! But…" Paula sighed. "I miss living closer to Tiya. I don't see her as much as I'd like to." At this, Elodie's eyes flicked to Tiya, who was enjoying an impromptu magic show by Oscar. "My contract requires that I stay with Bijou full-time, so Tiya lives with her dad to be closer to school and her friends. It's a sacrifice, but one I'm willing to make."

"Why?"

There was a pause on the other end of the line. "Monsieur Saint Martin loved Bijou more than anything. He raised her since she was a year old. All he wanted was for her to be happy, and he was willing to pay a lot to make sure that happened. Tiya will be able to go to any college she wants thanks to my job. She might not realize it, but Bijou is the best thing that's ever happened to us." Paula broke off. "Oh, my goodness, listen to me! You called to talk about Bijou, and here I am telling you my life's story." There was a rustle on Paula's end of the call, then the sound of traffic and a car door slamming. "I'm afraid I have to go. I'm at the florist. You should come to the party tonight. You can meet Bijou. Ask Tiya for an invitation! I left extras on the kitchen table."

Elodie said goodbye, hung up the phone, and went in search of the invitations. Printed on high-quality paper, it was obvious that no expense had been spared. A photograph of Bijou was on the right side of the invitation and beside it were the party details. It was signed "XO Bijou" and stamped with her pawprint.

Was it a coincidence that Bijou had gone missing so close to the party? The timing was suspicious. And the movie shoot couldn't resume until Bijou was found either. She was the star, after all. Elodie absent-mindedly drummed her fingers on the table and Carnegie trotted over. The insniffigation was complete. Elodie looked down at her dog, now seated and waiting for further instruction, or maybe a cuddle.

Elodie chose the latter and sat down beside Carnegie, who gave her a lick on the nose. "Someone took Bijou, but why? What was their motive?" Elodie asked, thinking out loud as she scratched the sweet spot under Carnegie's ear. "If we figure out the why, maybe that will lead us to the who."

Chapter 5
BIANCA

As Elodie deliberated her next steps, Oscar climbed to the top of the tallest cat tower and peered out the window at the courtyard below.

"Hey, Elodie, do you mind if I take a break?" Oscar asked. His face was pressed to the window. "I want to practice my parkour."

Elodie frowned. "Now? We've just started an investigation." She went to the window to see what had drawn his interest away from the case. A tall, solidly built man was in the middle of the courtyard talking with someone. It was Lance Beauregard, the stuntman.

"Now's my chance! Mom told me I couldn't bother him on set. But he's *technically* not on set if the movie's not filming today."

Investigation or not, Elodie couldn't stand in the way of Oscar meeting his idol—literally, because he didn't wait for Elodie's reply before he'd leapt from the cat tower and sprinted out the door.

Not to be deterred by Oscar's sudden disappearance, Elodie turned to Tiya. "Your mom mentioned Monsieur Saint Martin got Bijou when she was a year old. Do you know who owned her first?" A possible motive was formulating in Elodie's mind. Maybe Bijou's original owner regretted giving her up and wanted her back.

"It was his niece, Bianca."

"Bianca Winthrop Parker Saint Martin," Elodie stated. The name, though a mouthful, was well-known at The Biltmore. Bianca was

Lucien's niece. Determined not to rule anyone out until she questioned them, Elodie clipped Carnegie's leash onto her collar. "I'm going to interview Bianca. You need to stay here, close to the phone. It's possible the motive for Bijou's abduction was greed. If that's the case, the catnapper will want a ransom."

Tiya winced. "All I have is $38.27 in my savings account."

Elodie gave Tiya her most confident look. "Which is why the faster I figure out who took Bijou, the better."

If there was royalty at The Biltmore, it was the Winthrop Parkers of #11D. Generations of the well-known family had occupied the same apartment since The Biltmore had been erected in 1908.

When the elevator doors opened, Elodie found Bianca Winthrop Parker Saint Martin locking the door to her penthouse apartment.

Until Bijou came along, Bianca had been Lucien Saint Martin's muse. As a teenager, she'd walked his runway and accompanied him on his private plane to exotic locations. But Bijou's arrival had changed things, or that was how it seemed. Could Bianca have been jealous of Bijou? There was only one way to find out.

Elodie cleared her throat. "Bianca?"

"Yes," the young woman tossed her curtain of long, blond hair over her shoulder. "I was just on my way out."

"This won't take long," Elodie said. "I'm actually here because of Bijou. I'm writing an article about her for *The Biltmore Bulletin*." Elodie watched Bianca carefully. A guilty person would show signs of surprise, or even fear that they'd been found out. Bianca's face stayed placid.

"Bijou was your cat first. Why did you give her to your uncle?"

Bianca glanced at her watch and sat on the

settee outside the apartment door. She made space **and gestured** for Elodie to sit too.

"We were going out of town, skiing in Aspen, I think. Since Uncle Lucien lived in the building, I asked if he'd take her for the week. He didn't want to, at first. He was worried about cat hair and the litter box, but he adored me and couldn't say no." Bianca arched a well-groomed eyebrow. "The joke was on me though. When we came back, he told me Bijou was his. I think he described her as his 'soul mate.'"

"Were you angry? After all, she was your cat." Elodie glanced protectively at Carnegie who had just laid down at her feet, chin resting on her front paws.

"I guess I should have been, but while we were gone, Uncle Lucien had turned Bijou into an absolute princess. I never would have measured up. Plus," Bianca tilted her head, a wistful look on her face, "he was lonely. I liked that he had Bijou to keep him company. He was so sweet with her."

Bianca sounded sincere, not like a jealous, vengeful catnapper. Bianca stood up. Her curtain of hair fell like silk down her back. "Shall we?" she motioned to the elevator. Elodie agreed and shared a pleasant ride to the lobby. While the chat hadn't led to the culprit, at least she'd been able to cross a suspect off her list.

Chapter 6
ANTONIO

Elodie said a rushed goodbye to Bianca because the moment the elevator doors opened to the lobby, Carnegie spied one of her favorite people and dashed out. Freddy, now in his regular doorman's uniform of a well-cut vest and dapper hat, was chatting with someone unfamiliar to Elodie. Even though Freddy was in the middle of a conversation, he bent down to pat Carnegie who forgot all decorum and promptly rolled over for a belly rub.

Freddy frowned at the man who held a small voice recorder in Freddy's direction.

"I've already told you, Antonio, I've got nothing to say."

"Come on, Freddy. You're the doorman," he cajoled. "You must see things. You know everyone in the building. Don't worry, my sources are always anonymous." Antonio leaned in, eagerly.

Freddy shook his head, visibly gritting his teeth. "I'm not talking to you."

"Oh, come on. It's not like I'm the press. I'm an author. And besides," Antonio smirked, "I live here."

Since when? Elodie wondered. She'd never seen him before. Something about Antonio's slicked-back hair and dark tan reminded Elodie of the actors from the movie. He looked too smooth to be real.

Freddy drew up to his full height and stared down at Antonio. "All due respect, Antonio, but you *don't* live here. You're a temporary resident, renting an apartment while you research your book."

Elodie's curiosity was piqued now. *What book was Freddy talking about?*

It looked like Antonio wanted to argue, but Elodie stepped forward. "Excuse me, Freddy. Could you help me with something?"

Freddy nodded at Antonio, turned away, and faced Elodie.

"I owe you one," Freddy whispered once Antonio was out of earshot. "He's been hounding me for information since he moved in here."

"Who is he?"

"Antonio Altomare. He's staying in #2G while he writes his book."

"What's the book about?" Elodie asked.

"Bijou." Freddy laughed under his breath and shook his head. "A cat with her own biography. Imagine that! Guess it's harder to write an interesting book about a cat than he thought. He's trying to spice it up with gossip about The Biltmore." Freddy took in Elodie's notebook, and the bow tied around Carnegie's neck. "Let me guess. You're on a case and you need to scoot?"

Freddy's observations were correct, so he went to the storage room near his desk and returned with Elodie's scooter. "Oscar is already out there. That boy tore through the lobby like his hair was on fire!"

Elodie wheeled her scooter through the large doors that led to the courtyard. She needed to untangle what she'd learned so far about the case, and the best way to do that was to take her scooter for a spin around the courtyard, but first she needed to speak with Oscar.

Only, when she got to the courtyard, Oscar was nowhere to be found. Elodie walked around the entire space but saw no sign of him. The courtyard was unusually large for New York City, but not so large that someone could get lost. Had he gone back to his apartment? Had he been hurt? With Oscar's stunting, both options were equally possible. Elodie paused in front of the fountain where she'd spied Lance Beauregard from Bijou's apartment. Had Oscar gone somewhere with him?

"Oscar?" she called.

And then she heard it. A sniffle. Elodie spun around and spotted her friend tucked behind a boxwood. He was hurt! Elodie ran to him, followed by Carnegie who nosed her way through the dense shrub. "What happened?" Elodie asked, checking for blood or protruding bones. She'd never seen Oscar cry before.

"Nothing," Oscar said, wiping his nose.

Elodie tilted her head, surveying the scene. Her detective skills kicked in. Oscar had come to speak with Lance. He had no visible injuries but was clearly upset. "Is this about Lance?"

Oscar rolled his shoulders. "Yeah."

Elodie's heart sank for her friend. "What did he say?"

"To give up. He said stunting is a dead end and that cats get treated better than he does." Fat tears rolled down Oscar's cheeks. "Everything I've been working for has been a waste!"

Two things swirled in Elodie's mind. The first was advice Miss Rosa had given her when she wondered if clients would take someone her age seriously as a detective. Miss Rosa had assured her that they would if she took herself seriously. The second was that she shared Tiya's negative opinion about Lance. Not only was he jealous of Bijou but he'd also crushed her friend's dreams.

"It's time to get out of the boxwood hedge, Oscar," Elodie said, using her most authoritative voice. She half-dragged Oscar to his feet and dusted off the bark chips and dried-up leaves covering his legs. "If I can be a detective, you can be a stunt person. Who cares what Lance says? It's what you want that matters."

Elodie's words, or maybe her feisty support, bolstered Oscar's spirits. "Do you really think I could be a stunt person?"

Elodie gave an uncharacteristic snort. "I don't think, *I know*. And you already are. Look at what you can do in the courtyard."

"You mean, the par-kourtyard," he said with a sniffle.

"I'll sit here with Carnegie, and you can show me your latest moves," Elodie said, smoothing out her skirt before taking a seat on the bench. Elodie glanced at her scooter, wishing she could kick off and do a quick spin around the courtyard to organize her thoughts, but right now Oscar needed her. Detective, or not, she was a friend first.

After a few minutes of flipping, leaping, and bounding—and perhaps the wisdom of Elodie's words—Oscar was back to his old self.

"How'd the interview go with Bianca?" he asked, panting as he came to sit beside her.

Elodie went over everything she'd learned. "There's also this nosy writer looking for gossip. He was hounding Freddy."

"That Antonio guy? He was out here too. He wanted to know how Lance felt about working with Bijou. Said it was for a Bijou-ography."

"What did Lance say?" Elodie asked.

Oscar frowned. "He got kind of annoyed and said it was ridiculous for a cat to get this much attention, on set and in print."

With a sinking feeling in her stomach, Elodie realized that if jealousy was the motive, Oscar's former idol could be the prime suspect.

"Whose is this?" Elodie asked. She pried an empty box of allergy pills away from Carnegie, who'd chewed one end into a pulpy mess.

"They might be Lance's!" Oscar proclaimed. "Remember, Tiya said he was allergic to Bijou!"

Oscar was right. Elodie held the box in front of her face wondering if this was a helpful clue, or just garbage. It was time for Elodie to do some serious investigative thinking, so she picked up Carnegie and secured her in the scooter's basket. Elodie kicked off. Carnegie raised her nose in the air to better feel the rush of wind through her fur.

Elodie ran through everyone she'd met so far. Paula wasn't a suspect. Her job depended on Bijou, so it wasn't logical that she'd be the catnapper. Bianca had no motive. Lance may have been jealous of Bijou, but like Paula, his job depended on Bijou—the movie couldn't happen without her, plus, he was allergic to cats. It didn't seem reasonable he'd be the culprit.

Elodie felt a flash of envy towards Antonio, the writer. He could ask anyone anything he wanted. The mystery would have been easier to solve if Elodie had the same luxury. Keeping a case classified was difficult!

"Hey, Elodie, pick a card." Oscar jumped out in front of her scooter. He held a fanned-out deck of cards in his hands. Elodie wasn't in the mood for more of his magic tricks, but did as she was asked. She glanced at the card. "Now put it back." Elodie slid it into the middle of the deck. With a flourish, Oscar shuffled the cards. He tapped the top card with his finger and flipped it over to reveal Elodie's card. Despite feeling glum about the lack of progress and the looming deadline in the catnapping case, Elodie grinned.

"How'd you do that?"

"A magician never reveals his tricks," Oscar said. "But I will tell you this, it's all about distraction." He gave a knowing wink. "While you were watching the deck, I was making the magic happen."

"You distracted me," Elodie said slowly, narrowing her eyes. *Distraction. Was that the key to this mystery?* Elodie thought about what she'd learned so far. She'd been focused on Bijou's disappearance which was exactly what the clever catnapper had wanted her to do.

She quickly unclipped Carnegie and lifted

her from the basket. "Thank you, Oscar! Your magic trick may have solved this case!"

"What? It did?" Oscar hurried after Elodie as she beelined for the lobby.

"Yes! The catnapping is a distraction! If I'm correct, the catnapper is more interested in getting back at Paula than Bijou!" The best part about this new theory was that Elodie already had a suspect in mind: the person who'd admitted to being furious at Paula. "We need to visit Tiya."

Elodie explained her theory to Oscar as they made their way to the elevator. "Tiya told us that Paula would lose her job if Bijou went missing, which is exactly what Tiya wants."

Elodie expected Oscar to jump on board and agree with her. Instead, he frowned. "Hang on," he said, blocking her from pressing the Up button. "I don't think Tiya's lying to us. Sure, she was jealous of Bijou, but she was also really upset when she found out the cat was missing, and she was worried that her mom would think she was responsible. She doesn't want her mom to find out, remember?"

"But…" Elodie drifted off, grasping for threads to stitch her theory back together. "She told us about their argument." *I wish Bijou would disappear*. Those had been Tiya's exact words. "If her mom lost her job, she'd have to move back to Queens."

"Oh-kay," Oscar said, drawing the word out. "Then why come to us for help? And what'd she do with Bijou? The cat's not in her apartment. It just doesn't make sense."

Elodie sighed, realizing Oscar was right. She'd let her desperation for a suspect cloud her judgment. Thank goodness Oscar had stopped her from making a foolish accusation.

"But if someone *else* wanted to make Paula look bad…" Oscar's eyes lit up.

Elodie's mind clicked through possibilities. One door may have closed, but Oscar's astute observation had opened another. "It's been hours since the catnapping and there's been no ransom note, which makes it unlikely Bijou was taken for the money. But if the cat was taken to get back at Paula…what better time to do it than before the big party."

Oscar leaned over to press the button for the elevator. "You're right about one thing: we do need to talk to Tiya. If anyone knows about who'd do something like this to her mom, it'll be her."

The doors slid open. Oscar, Carnegie, and Elodie stepped on and just as the doors were nearly closed a figure darted past. Someone had been eavesdropping! Elodie pressed the button to open the doors, but it was too late. The elevator had started its ascent. Elodie's stomach, on the other hand, plummeted. Tiya had asked for one thing: secrecy. And now, Elodie had let the cat out of the bag.

Chapter 7
RAMON

"No one's called," Tiya said when they arrived at Bijou's apartment. "That's a good thing, right?"

"It fits with our new theory," Elodie said, examining the list of names, phone numbers, and addresses titled 'Bijou's Staff' hanging on the fridge. The best place to find someone who might want to get back at Paula would be here.

"Have any of these people been in arguments with your mom?" Elodie asked Tiya.

Tiya's fingernails were even more chewed up than before. As they spoke, she fidgeted with one of Bijou's tiny, rhinestone-studded bows. Elodie recognized it as the type given to Spaw clients.

"I don't know if I'd call it an argument exactly, but I heard Ramon, the trainer, telling someone on set that he should be getting paid more for what he does with Bijou. He said something like, 'All Paula does is clean the litter box and she gets to live in a three-bed, two-bath on the tenth floor.' He sounded kind of jealous. As soon as he realized I'd overheard, he rushed away."

Elodie opened her investigation diary and located the card Mrs. Fineman had dropped in the elevator. "He lives in #1E."

Oscar arched an eyebrow. "Sounds like we need to pay Ramon a visit."

Ramon's apartment was on the ground floor where the units were smaller and less desirable. Originally built as physician's offices, they all had small windows and low ceilings. The only view was of foot traffic on 78th St. It was no wonder Ramon was jealous of Paula's accommodation. Elodie straightened Carnegie's bow and ran her hand over her dog's back. Any professional animal trainer would take one look at Carnegie and realize she was not in need of training, but all Elodie needed was a few moments with Ramon. If he was the catnapper, she was sure she'd be able to tell. He'd be surprised at the unannounced visitors, shifty if they asked to come in, and defensive about what he'd been up to that morning. Her parents had explained that often it wasn't the theft that led to a thief's downfall, it was the pressure of hiding the crime.

Carnegie's ears perked up at the sound of heavy footsteps inside the apartment. Ramon opened the door. He'd aged since the photo on his business card. A heavy-set man, his curls were more gray than black, and he had a very thick mustache.

Ramon looked from Elodie to Oscar and down to Carnegie. He bent down to let Carnegie sniff his hand. "Who's this?" he asked, running a hand over her head and under her chin.

"This is Carnegie. Are you Ramon, the animal trainer?" Elodie asked.

"I am, but I'm not taking any new clients right now," he said, standing up and smiling down at Carnegie.

"Oh," Elodie's face fell. "Paula sent us. She said you'd be able to help." Elodie's chest twinged at the lie, even though it was a tiny one and necessary to the case. Time was of the essence. Until Bijou was found, Elodie was determined to do what she must, even if it meant stretching the truth.

"Paula? Bijou's nanny?"

Elodie watched Ramon's face carefully. "She said you 'worked wonders with Bijou.' Those were her exact words."

Ramon's cheeks flushed.

"Yeah. And she said that if anyone could help Carnegie, it was you," Oscar added. "Paula's a real fan."

"Huh? News to me," Ramon muttered under his breath.

"Really?" Elodie gave Oscar a sidelong glance. Was this the break they'd been waiting for?

Ramon ran a hand through his hair. There were several long scratches on his forearm. "What happened?" she asked, pointing at them. The cuts looked fresh.

"Occupational hazard," Ramon said with a shrug. "Look, thanks for coming by, but I'm actually working with a client right now." He'd almost shut the door when Carnegie's tail shot straight up. Something inside had caught her attention.

"What is it, Carnegie?" Elodie whispered. Her dog whimpered and strained at the leash. Had Carnegie caught the scent of something suspicious? Elodie dropped the leash and Carnegie darted between Ramon's legs and into the apartment.

"What the—?" As Ramon turned to watch the Westie, Oscar dropped to his stomach and army crawled past Ramon. Elodie leaned in, listening, and heard the same noise Carnegie had.

A cat's meow.

Elodie rushed inside. Carnegie was standing on her hind legs in front of the kitchen table, barking. On top of the table was a cat carrier. Inside the cat carrier was none other than Bijou!

Elodie rounded on Ramon. "You're the catnapper!"

"Catnapper?" Ramon sputtered. "What are you talking about?"

"You know what we're talking about. Bijou went missing earlier today and you're the one who took her!" Oscar jabbed a finger in Ramon's direction.

Ramon crossed his arms over his chest, unfazed. "I did not. What kind of an animal trainer steals his own clients? I'd be out of business in a New York minute."

Oscar scoffed. "Oh yeah? Well, explain *that*." Oscar pointed at the cat. "Did she walk here herself? Admit it, we caught you red-handed."

Ramon looked at Oscar and Elodie exasperated. "That isn't Bijou. It's Phoebe, her stunt double."

There was a long moment of silence. "Stunt double?" Oscar repeated, slowly.

"That's right. All stars have them, even the animals. Phoebe's fees are half of Bijou's and she's easier to work with. No imported shrimp for this old girl."

Elodie found the party invitation in her investigation diary. She held the card up to the cat in the carrier for comparison. While the cats had the same blue eyes and creamy fur, the markings around Phoebe's face were slightly different. Elodie didn't need to do a pawprint analysis to know Ramon was telling the truth.

Ramon pulled out a chair and sat down, eye level with Elodie. "Now, what do you mean, Bijou was taken?" A heaviness settled in Elodie's chest. The truth was out. "If she's missing, you need to tell the police."

"We promised Tiya we wouldn't," Oscar said.

"Tiya? Paula's daughter?"

Oscar nodded. "If anyone finds out, Paula will lose her job."

"Well, if Bijou isn't found, we will all lose

our jobs. This isn't the kind of secret you're supposed to keep. And, no offense, but you're just a kid, not a detective." It wasn't the first time someone had decided her age determined her ability. Usually, she knew they were wrong, but with this case, she wasn't so sure. She had no leads, no suspects, and was running out of time.

"Actually, she's a kid *and* a detective," Oscar said, jumping to Elodie's defense. "And she's Bijou's best hope. The New York Police Department have more important things to do than look for a missing cat." Ramon couldn't argue with that, but he still didn't look convinced that the LaRue Detective Agency was up to the task.

"You've got one hour. If you haven't found Bijou by then, I'm calling someone who can."

Chapter 8
ALFIE

Elodie and Oscar went to the courtyard to mull things over. Well, Elodie was mulling. Oscar was practicing tricks on his unicycle.

"You could get your scooter again," Oscar suggested.

Elodie shook her head. She wasn't sure a few more spins around the courtyard could solve this problem. She'd never hit a dead end like this before. Tucked behind the cover of her investigation diary was a card with the phone number for Officers Hyland and Zubick of the New York Police Department. The two policemen had seen Elodie's sleuthing skills in action before. If she needed them, they were a phone call away. The question was: did she need them?

Was it time to tell Tiya this case was too much for the LaRue Detective Agency? On the other side of the courtyard, Oscar tumbled into a boxwood hedge. The same one he'd been hiding behind after Lance had dashed his dreams. Oscar was up in a flash. "I'm good!" he called and gave her a thumbs up.

Her advice to Oscar about not listening to Lance had been sound, but here she was, struggling with doubts about *her* abilities.

"How are things going, Elodie?" Freddy strolled over. His doorman's cap sat at a jaunty angle on his head.

"Not great," Elodie sighed, staring at the officers' phone number. "I'm stumped on a case. I might have to," she could barely get the words out, "drop it." Elodie's reasoning and sharp eyes had helped her solve cases in the past, but this time she was in the dark. It was as mystifying as one of Oscar's magic tricks. She had to face the possibility that it was time to admit defeat.

Freddy raised his eyebrows. "Drop it? That doesn't sound like you."

"I've considered all the angles and interviewed suspects. Nothing is making sense. It's like a puzzle piece is missing and until I find it, I can't make things fit."

The conversation was cut short by raised voices in the lobby. "What is going on?" Freddy muttered, jumping up. He smoothed his vest and tugged his shirt sleeves tight. "I'll be right back," he said and rushed off.

Normally, Elodie would have been curious too, but not in her current mood. She'd gone from mulling to moping. Her parents often said that detectives were only as good as their last case. Their last *successfully solved* case.

Elodie sighed and looked once more at the business card for Officers Hyland and Zubick. Her mind was made up. She was going to tell Tiya that the LaRue Detective Agency was quitting the catnapping case and advise her to call the police.

"Are you sure?" Oscar asked after Elodie explained her decision. He peddled around her in circles as she and Carnegie walked back toward the building. "Ramon gave us an hour. We've still got time."

But as they reached the lobby door, Elodie saw that Oscar was wrong—they did *not* have time.

Paula was back from her errands! She carried bags bulging with groceries, flowers, and twenty helium balloons. In front of her stood a man in a linen suit. His face was flushed red with anger. Oscar jumped off his unicycle and rested it against the building. Elodie and Oscar slipped inside the lobby, tucking themselves behind a wingback chair, and listened to the exchange.

There was no yelling, thanks to Freddy's presence, but things were still heated. The man pointed a finger in Paula's face. "When were you planning on telling me about Bijou?"

"Telling you what, Alfie?"

Elodie's heart thudded in her chest. She didn't need to look in her investigation diary to confirm that Alfie was Bijou's agent. She held her breath, waiting to hear what he said next.

"The cat is missing!"

Oscar gaped at Elodie. How had Alfie found out?

Paula set down the bags, wiping the back of her hand across her forehead. She looked worn out from the summer heat and a busy day of running errands. "Bijou's not missing. She had her weekly appointment at Spaw. I sent Tiya to pick her up a few hours ago."

Just then, the elevator's ding announced its arrival. The doors slid open. "Mom?" Tiya squeaked in surprise. "You're back!"

Paula gave an exhausted smile. "Alfie was

just asking about Bijou. You picked her up, right?"

Tiya opened her mouth but didn't get a word out before Alfie answered for her. "She didn't. It's all right here!" He held up a poster, the kind that got taped to lampposts. From where Elodie stood, she could see the headline. 'Bijou Be Gone!' "These are up all over the neighborhood!"

Paula dropped the groceries and flowers. Freddy had the sense to grab the balloons before they floated to the ceiling and got tangled in the chandelier. "Let me see that." Ripping the paper out of Alfie's hands, Paula read it out loud.

Get Caught In the Web Of the UPPER WEST SPY-DER!

BIJOU BE GONE

by the Upper West Spy-der

EXCLUSIVE: The world's wealthiest feline, Bijou Saint Martin, has been catnapped! An anonymous source close to the cat confirms she was snatched this morning from local salon, Spaw. Her current whereabouts are unknown.

How could such a crime occur?

The abduction has left many questioning the level of care the cat has received following Lucien Saint Martin's death. Paula Benson, Bijou's nanny, could not be reached for comment, but she was spotted earlier today shopping on Madison Avenue...unaware that the cat was missing? Or maybe she just doesn't care? Despite living in the lap of luxury, sources have overheard Paula complaining about her job. Perhaps it's a blessing that Lucien Saint Martin isn't around to see the cat-atrophic way his beloved Bijou is being treated.

Bijou has been filming a movie and was supposed to celebrate her eighth birthday tonight with a lavish party at the illustrious Biltmore on West Broadway. Will the feline film star be found in time? And if she isn't, what will it mean for the movie? For answers to these questions and more, keep your eyes peeled for the next installment of the Upper West Spy-der!

"Who wrote this?" Paula stammered. "Who is the Upper West Spy-der?"

Alfie snatched the paper back. "I don't care who wrote it! What I want to know is where's Bijou?"

Paula and Alfie both turned to the only person who could answer. "I'm sorry, Mom," Tiya said and burst into tears.

Elodie's heart sank for her. This was exactly the moment Tiya had wanted to avoid by asking for Elodie's help, and by not solving the case in time, Elodie had failed her.

"I don't know where Bijou is. When I got to Spaw, she was gone!"

"Unbelievable!" Alfie fumed. "Asking a child to do your job. No wonder the cat is missing!" He threw his arms up in exasperation.

"Who leaked the story?" Oscar whispered. "Was it Ramon? Besides us, he's the only person who knew about the catnapping."

The truth sat like a hard lump in Elodie's stomach. "Ramon's not the leak. The article wouldn't benefit him at all. I'm the leak." Oscar gaped at her. Tiya's number one request had been discretion. Elodie had made the mistake of discussing the case in the lobby and had been overheard. "Whoever was eavesdropping on our conversation by the elevator wrote this article, Oscar." Their attention was pulled back to Paula and Alfie, who were still arguing.

"Alfie, I'm sure if we take a minute to think this through—" Paula started, but Alfie cut her off.

"Take a minute! We don't have a minute! Have you forgotten about what's happening tonight? How are we going to throw a party for Bijou when Bijou's not here? I'm calling the police," he said, crumpling the Upper West Spy-der's article.

Alfie stormed towards the front doors. "Hello? 911? I need the police. A cat is missing. Yes, a *cat*! Hello? Hello!"

Paula looked at the groceries, flowers, and supplies, and then at Freddy who was still behind her holding the balloons. She bent down to pick up the Zabar's bags when Tiya grabbed her hand. "Mom, I'm so sorry!"

"Hush, Titi," Paula said, sharply, scanning the lobby. "What matters right now is finding Bijou. I just hope—" she broke off for a moment. "I hope Bijou is okay." The shocking news of Bijou's abduction seemed to wash over her. Paula pressed her lips together. "Let's get upstairs so I can figure out what I need to do." She looked at her daughter and frowned, dropping her voice. "I wish you had told me right away. I could lose my job over this."

Tiya erupted into fresh tears. "I know! That's why I wanted to fix it."

"Fix it how?"

Elodie knew this was her moment to step forward, but she hesitated. She'd made a mess of things. How could she claim to be a detective? She hadn't solved the case and she'd also breached her client's privacy. Now all of the Upper West Side knew Bijou was missing.

The only way to salvage her reputation was to take responsibility, so Elodie cleared her throat and said, "By hiring the LaRue Detective Agency."

Paula turned to Elodie. "LaRue? Are you the one who interviewed me?" Elodie squirmed. She hadn't been completely honest during the interview and now the lie had caught up with her. The truth, or most of it, was out now anyway. There was no point in keeping more secrets.

"Yes. This is Oscar and Carnegie, my dog. We've been investigating Bijou's disappearance."

Paula turned to Tiya, incredulous. "You hired a detective?"

Tiya nodded and cast a hopeful look in Elodie's direction. "She's the best in the building. I felt so bad about saying I wished Bijou would disappear. You know I didn't mean it."

"Of course, I know that. But if we don't find Bijou, my *job* will disappear." Paula tilted her daughter's chin up so they could meet eye to eye. "This was not a secret you should have kept, but, as much as I hate to admit it, Alfie's right. I shouldn't have asked you to pick up Bijou. That was my job, not yours. I thought being here for the movie and the party would be fun for you, but I was wrong about that too, wasn't I?" Paula looked lovingly at Tiya and pulled her into a hug.

Oscar nudged Elodie with his elbow. They might not have solved the case, but it felt like some good had come out of their investigation. As Paula and Tiya reached down for the bags of party supplies, Elodie remembered something—a clue that hadn't seemed important before but could be now.

She tucked the card with Officer Zubick and Hyland's number back into her investigation diary and flipped back a few pages. "Oscar," she said quietly, but urgently, "I have an idea, but we'll need Miss Rosa's help."

Chapter 9
MISS ROSA

Oscar and Elodie found Miss Rosa in the apartment washing paintbrushes in the laundry room sink. It was a cramped space, made smaller with a variety of rags drying on racks and brushes sticking out of paint-spattered jars. Oscar leapt onto the washing machine and attempted to scale a cupboard before Miss Rosa yanked him back to the ground.

"We've made some progress on the case," Elodie announced. "We're close to solving it, but we need to do some more fieldwork. Some *off-site* fieldwork."

Miss Rosa raised her eyebrows, intrigued. "Where?"

Instead of answering, Elodie grabbed the reusable shopping bags from the basket in the front hall closet and clipped Carnegie's leash back on her collar. She'd made a regrettable blunder and had some doubt-filled moments, but she was back on track. The catnapping case was still hers to solve. "Grab your grocery list and follow me."

Once a week, Miss Rosa, Elodie, and Carnegie went to Zabar's. Like The Biltmore, the family-run grocery store and deli had been around for over a hundred years. It was a neighborhood mainstay and because Elodie had been coming here since she was a little girl she was given special treatment. She got samples at the deli from Jose, a pinch on the cheek from Myrna in the bakery, and Carnegie got a treat from the butcher.

Today, while Miss Rosa wove her way through the narrow aisles to do her shopping, Elodie and Oscar went to the fish counter. Seeing Paula with her grocery bags had reminded Elodie of something Tiya had mentioned about Bijou's eating habits: only the most expensive shrimp would do and there was only one place to get it.

"Hello," Elodie said to the man behind the fish counter. She wasn't tall enough to see over the top of it, but the man leaned over the glass to peer down at her. Smoked salmon of all varieties, fresh fish fillets, scallops, and shrimp lay in orderly rows under the glass. A smell that can best be described as fishy hung in the air.

"What can I help you with?"

"Do you sell gambas rojas de Dénia?" Elodie asked, referring to the notes in her investigation diary about Bijou's favorite food.

The man bent to peer at what laid under the glass. "We do, but we're sold out."

Elodie's heart quickened. "Can you tell me who bought them?"

"I just started my shift. Let me ask Julien. He's been here since we opened."

By now, Oscar had put two and two together. He and Elodie stood shoulder to shoulder on their tiptoes watching as a different man emerged from the back room. "You the kids asking about the gambas rojas de Dénia?" the words rolled off his tongue in perfectly accented Spanish.

"Yes."

Julien leaned against the counter. "We special order it for someone. A lady." Elodie nodded. He meant Paula, of course. "This morning someone else came in and tried to buy a bunch. I could only sell a few pieces because the regular customer was coming by later."

Elodie shot Oscar a triumphant look. They were closing in on the catnapper! "What do you remember about the person from this morning?"

"Anything's helpful," Oscar added. "Was it a man or a woman?"

Julien pulled his eyebrows together thinking. "I don't remember. I know people by their orders, not what they look like. You know, one guy gets half a pound of smoked salmon every Thursday. Another lady gets a container of whitefish salad, that kind of thing."

"Do you remember what else the customer bought?" Elodie asked. It was a long shot, but maybe it would turn into a clue.

Julien scratched his forehead thinking. "Now that you mention it, yeah." When Elodie heard what Julien had to say, everything fell into place. "That's it, Oscar! I've cracked this catnapping case!"

Chapter 10
LAWRENCE

It was so obvious, Elodie couldn't believe she hadn't seen it before.

Upon returning to The Biltmore, Elodie and Oscar bid Miss Rosa adieu outside of #5D. Elodie pressed the button for the eighth floor. "You're sure you want to do this?" Oscar asked doubtfully.

"Absolutely!" Elodie's earlier uncertainty was gone. The new suspect had motive and opportunity. All Elodie and Oscar had to do was retrieve Bijou to prove it.

The elevator doors opened and Elodie bounded out with Carnegie and Oscar close behind. She was rarely this excited to nab a culprit, but with all her misgivings finally put to rest, Elodie couldn't wait to bring Bijou home. "Allow me," Oscar said gallantly and rapped three times on the door to #8F. A high-pitched yapping began on the other side of the door.

Lawrence lunged for them the second Mrs. Fineman opened the door. He barked and darted around Oscar and Elodie's legs. Carnegie's tail went up, allowing for a sniff of her hindquarters. "Come, Lawrence," Mrs. Fineman commanded and held out some of the stinky freeze-dried herring. The same treat Julien had sold with the gambas rojas de Dénia. "Yes?" she said. "What do you want?" Mrs. Fineman, with Lawrence at her side, stood like a sentry barring their view of the apartment beyond.

Elodie hesitated. Good manners made it

difficult for her to enter without an invitation. Luckily, Oscar had no such qualms. "Whoa! Is that an original Harry Houdini poster?" he asked, barging past Mrs. Fineman and Lawrence.

Mrs. Fineman, surprised by Oscar's interest, didn't comment on his intrusion, but followed him inside. "Yes. My grandfather was his manager. You know who Harry Houdini was?"

"Only the greatest magician ever!" Oscar said and gave an almost imperceptible nod of his head to Elodie. Her cue to start snooping! While Oscar peppered Mrs. Fineman with questions, Elodie and Carnegie went on the prowl for Bijou. The cat had to be here somewhere!

Mrs. Fineman's two-bedroom apartment was filled with books. It looked more like a library than a home. A large oil painting of Lawrence occupied the space over the buffet in the dining room. The spare room had been turned into an office. Mrs. Fineman's computer sat on a large desk. Behind it, an issue of the first *Biltmore Bulletin* hung on the wall.

Elodie jumped as a wet nose nudged her leg. She looked down to see not Carnegie, but Lawrence. Mrs. Fineman might have been busy with Oscar, but Lawrence wasn't going to let Elodie and her dog look around unaccompanied. It appeared that he had free reign of the apartment; no doors were closed, which made Elodie wonder where Mrs. Fineman had stashed Bijou. Surely Lawrence would have raised a ruckus if a cat showed up in his home.

"One *last* question," Oscar said loudly from the living room. A signal for Elodie to wrap things up.

No, Elodie thought, frustrated. *Bijou has to be here!* She looked down at Lawrence. She was running out of time and ideas. "Do you know?" she asked Lawrence. He stared up at her, panting. It was a stretch, and she felt ridiculous, but she found herself doing it anyway. "Where's the cat, Lawrence?"

To her surprise, Lawrence trotted over to a closet and pawed at the door. Elodie followed. "In here?" she whispered. "Is the cat in here?"

Lawrence whimpered.

Holding her breath, Elodie began to open the door.

"What are you doing?" Mrs. Fineman's voice made Elodie jump. "That cupboard is off-limits!" Elodie spun around to see Mrs. Fineman marching toward her, followed by Oscar. "All of Lawrence's treats are in there and he's on a diet. Aren't you?" she peered at her dog who wagged his tail hopefully.

This sure thing had turned into another dead-end.

"I suppose you can have one more," Mrs. Fineman said, smiling at her dog. "But only because you're such a good boy." She swung open the door the rest of the way. Sure enough, the shelves were filled with treats, but no cat. Without Bijou, Elodie had no proof that Mrs. Fineman was behind the catnapping.

Elodie, Carnegie, and Oscar turned to go. "Was there a reason you came by?" Mrs. Fineman asked, picking Lawrence up.

"We, uh…" Elodie's mind was blank. What reason could she possibly give?

"We want to write for *The Biltmore Bulletin*!" Oscar said, jumping to Elodie's rescue.

"Oh," Mrs. Fineman looked taken aback. "Well, that would be lovely. A fresh perspective is always a good idea."

As Mrs. Fineman showed them out, Elodie couldn't help but wonder about the shrimp. Had Mrs. Fineman bought them? Or was it someone else?

The ruses and undercover work hadn't gotten her very far with the investigation. Maybe it was time to ask a direct question. What did she have to lose?

"Did you buy gambas rojas de Dénia at Zabar's today?" Elodie asked.

Mrs. Fineman widened her eyes in surprise. "How did you know that?"

"It's a long story," Oscar said. "I can tell you if you want." He took a deep breath as if what he had to say would take a while.

Mrs. Fineman held up a hand, pausing him. "That's quite alright. I don't need to know. As for the shrimp, I've had some…regrets about my comments of late. I decided to buy a birthday gift for Bijou. Sort of an apology so we can start fresh."

"That's really nice, Mrs. Fineman," Oscar said. "I bet Bijou will love them."

Elodie gave a weak smile. In her head, she added, *If she ever gets them*.

Elodie hung her head in disappointment. She'd gone into #8F sure that Bijou would be on the other side of the door, and now here they were, leaving empty-handed. Discovering that Mrs. Fineman wasn't the culprit had been yet another blow to her confidence. Was she cut out for this line of work?

"Can you believe it? She had all kinds of Houdini artifacts. The secret handcuffs. A model of Q the Robot. Even a straight jacket, but she wouldn't let me try it on. Mrs. Fineman is not what I expected. I'm going back tomorrow so she can show me the publicity posters Houdini used," Oscar said excitedly as they walked to the elevator. "Houdini was the master of publicity. He used to challenge store owners to build a box he couldn't escape from, and then he did, every time! He had a disappearing elephant too. He'd fire a pistol and Jennie the Elephant would disappear." A strange look crossed Oscar's face. "Hey, you don't think Bijou is missing because of magic, do you?"

Elodie sighed. "No, but I wish I could use magic to solve it."

"No, you don't," Oscar said. "You're a detective through and through. You see things other people miss and figure out how all the clues go together. That's better than magic!"

Oscar's words were the vote of confidence Elodie needed. "Oscar, you're right. There's something we're missing and I'm not going to give up until I figure out what it is."

Elodie opened her investigation diary. One piece of evidence called to her. She hadn't thought much about it at first, but now she saw her mistake. "To the lobby!" she said and charged ahead with Carnegie at her heels and Oscar cartwheeling behind.

Chapter 11
UPPER WEST SPY-DER

Elodie and Oscar arrived in the lobby. Word of Bijou's disappearance had spread. Freddy put the phone down and looked at Elodie exasperated. "That Upper West Spy-der article has everyone worrying about their pets!" He lowered his voice. "And you should hear what people are saying about Paula."

Elodie frowned as Freddy's phone rang again. "Tell them the article is all lies. Bijou is fine and will be at her party. In fact," she glanced at Oscar as she said the next part, "tell them the party has been moved to the courtyard."

"Are you sure that's a good idea?" Oscar whispered. "It's a big risk. Paula will look even worse if Bijou isn't there."

"Not to worry, Oscar. I know who we're after and how we're going to catch them. Having all the residents at the party is essential to nabbing the catnapper." Elodie met his troubled gaze with a confident nod. There had been so many false leads and failed theories, Oscar wasn't wrong to doubt her. How *did* she know she was correct this time?

She opened her investigation diary and showed him the Upper West Spy-der article, which she'd reread in the elevator. There was one line in particular that jumped out at her. "Whoever wrote this article is also the catnapper. I may have said too much by the elevators, but I didn't say that."

Tiya's face fell when she answered the door and saw Elodie, Carnegie, and Oscar, but no Bijou. "You still haven't found her." She gave a hopeless sigh, but it didn't dampen Elodie's spirit.

"Not *yet*," Elodie replied. "But we're getting closer. The next few hours will be essential to bringing Bijou home."

"You know who took Bijou?" Paula joined Tiya at the door.

"No," Elodie admitted and then quickly added, "But I have a hunch, and I know how we're going to catch the culprit. All you have to do is what you were always going to do— throw a party for Bijou."

Paula looked skeptical. "Without Bijou?"

"Yes, because we *do* have Bijou," Oscar said.

"Elodie just said you don't have Bijou!" Tiya said, her exasperation growing.

The idea for Elodie's plan had come from watching Oscar perform magic tricks. Without giving away his secrets, he had explained that magicians, like Harry Houdini, made people see what they wanted them to. "It's all about tricking the eye," Oscar explained. Which was exactly what they were going to do to fool the catnapper into thinking Bijou had been found. "As long as you and Tiya behave normally, we can bring Bijou back to where she belongs."

Word quickly spread about Bijou's party. What had been a relatively intimate affair for friends, family, and castmates had turned into an open invitation for all of The Biltmore residents. Tables were set up for the food, drink, and ice sculptures. Balloons were tied to benches, and floral arrangements decorated the standing cocktail tables. In less than an hour, the space was transformed. First to arrive was Mr. Futterman, one of Elodie's most favorite residents at The Biltmore. His pet bird, a conure named Emerald, perched on his shoulder. He blew air kisses to Paula. "I'm so glad Bijou is safe," he said.

"So are we!" Paula replied. "I don't know why the Upper West Spy-der would write those lies."

"It's shocking what some people will do for attention," he tsked and gave Carnegie a pat on the head. More guests arrived. The question on everyone's lips was 'Where was Bijou?' but Elodie remained mum on the subject, assuring the guests that the cat of the hour would make her appearance as planned.

Mrs. Fineman, with Lawrence tucked under her arm, didn't look much happier about the party than she had been about the courtyard being used for the movie set, but she handed Paula a platter with the gambas rojas de Dénia. "For Bijou," she said. "I heard they're her favorite. I'm so relieved she's been found. I know how special pets are." The shrimp might have been on ice, but there was real warmth in Mrs. Fineman's peace offering.

Elodie stood off to the side, observing the guests and waiting for just the right moment to put her plan into action. "Is she really coming?" Another neighbor, Mrs. Vanderhoff, asked, cornering Paula.

Paula smiled, placidly. Elodie had to commend her for an excellent performance. "You know Bijou. She loves to make an entrance."

Speaking of entrances, Oscar narrowed his eyes and glared at the latest arrival. Lance Beauregard had just walked in. Oscar had taken it upon himself to provide entertainment. A small crowd had gathered to watch his impromptu magic show. But as soon as Lance walked past, Oscar fumbled his deck of cards and a ball that was supposed to stay hidden rolled out of his shirt sleeve. "Some magician you are," Antonio snorted as Oscar, red-faced with embarrassment, dropped to the ground to collect his things.

The chatter stopped as the DJ began

playing "Happy Birthday." Anticipation filled the air. Everyone was waiting for Bijou to appear and prove the Upper West Spy-der's article fit for the litter box.

Freddy held the door open for Ramon, who walked into the courtyard first, carrying a three-layer cake lit with eight candles. Bijou's name was spelled out in marquee letters. Behind Ramon, Paula carried a pink silk pillow and on that pillow was a cat with aqua eyes, creamy fur, and markings the color of a lightly toasted marshmallow around her face.

It was Bijou! At last! The crowd burst into applause.

But Elodie wasn't looking at the cat, and neither was Oscar. They had their eyes trained on their prime suspect. Just as they expected, the moment Bijou arrived the suspect's jaw dropped with disbelief. That was when Elodie knew, without a shadow of a doubt, that not only had the deception worked, but that she'd been right about the identity of the catnapper.

The suspect, eager to escape the courtyard, inched toward the lobby doors and—unnoticed by anyone but Elodie—slipped inside and headed straight for the elevator. Elodie waited until the elevator doors had slid shut, then she rushed toward the stairs. She knew exactly where the suspect was headed. Carnegie, excited by all the activity, bounded ahead. At the stairwell doors to the second floor, Elodie paused and waited. When she heard the *ding* of the elevator, she nudged the door open and watched the catnapper run out of the elevator.

The plan was working perfectly!

Timing was everything and Elodie held her breath waiting for the suspect to unlock the apartment door. "Go, Carnegie," she whispered and let her dog off the leash. In a flash, the Westie tore down the hallway, straight for the suspect.

Oscar's earlier fumble during his magic show had been a distraction. While on the ground, he'd used sleight of hand, the French Drop to be exact, to put a dog treat into the suspect's pant cuff. And now Carnegie, the seasoned insniffigator that she was, could smell it. Elodie bit back a grin as Carnegie twisted through the suspect's legs, sniffing at his ankles, and tying him up.

"What's going on?" The suspect hopped out of Carnegie's way but that only turned things into a game. Carnegie clamped down on the cuff where the treat was hidden. Not only had she found her treat, she'd apprehended the suspect too. Antonio Altomare wasn't going anywhere.

"Hey! Is this your dog?" he called to Elodie as she came down the hall. "Get her off me!" Antonio tried to shake his pant leg out of Carnegie's jaws, but the feisty terrier hung on. Even if Elodie had wanted to reign in Carnegie, she probably couldn't have. Not with a treat on the line. "What're you doing here, anyway? You don't live on this floor."

"I came to rescue Bijou."

Antonio's face paled under his fake tan. "What are you talking about? The cat's downstairs at that party." But the nervous glance inside his apartment told a different story.

"That's not Bijou. It's Phoebe, Bijou's stunt double. The real Bijou is in your apartment." Elodie's voice rang with triumph.

"What? That's ridiculous! Pfft," Antonio blew out a puff of air and tried once again to extricate the cuff of his pants from Carnegie's teeth. The little dog held on and growled. "You don't know what you're talking about!" Antonio sputtered. "You're not a detective. You're just a kid! You're—"

Antonio was interrupted by a wailing meow inside his apartment.

"Correct as usual, Elodie." Tall, lanky Officer Zubick said, emerging from the custodian's closet across from #2G. He was followed by his shorter, dark-haired partner, Officer Hyland. They'd been waiting in that hiding spot since the party started and had heard everything.

"Anything you want to tell us about what we'll find in there?" Officer Hyland asked, nodding at Antonio's apartment. The meows had turned into a caterwauling.

Antonio's shoulders slumped as he realized he'd been caught red-handed. "I was only going to keep her for a day or two."

"He needed to spice up Bijou's biography and what better way to do that than with a catnapping." When Antonio didn't argue, Elodie continued. "His plan backfired when Tiya kept Bijou's abduction a secret. He'd been counting on a media frenzy. But that didn't happen, so you wrote about it yourself." Elodie pulled out the Upper West Spy-der article. "You got lucky when you overheard me talking about the case."

Carnegie's determination paid off as she finally wrestled the treat from Antonio's cuff.

Antonio stepped aside as Elodie, Carnegie, and the police officers entered the apartment. Bijou's loud meows led Elodie and the officers to the guest bathroom.

Elodie opened the door. Bijou sat in the sink, still regal despite the cramped conditions. As soon as she saw Elodie she meowed again, but this time it was quieter and filled with gratitude. Elodie scooped her up. Bijou rubbed her cheek against Elodie's neck. It didn't matter that she was a dog person at heart, with Bijou in her arms, Elodie couldn't help falling a little in love with her.

In the living room, Antonio sat on the couch with his head in his hands. His plan had been thwarted and now he was out of a job.

"Another case closed," Officer Zubick said, slapping his notepad shut.

"Wish they were all this easy," Officer Hyland replied, hauling Antonio to his feet so he could be brought down to the station. They had more police work to do, but Elodie's mission was complete. She'd found Bijou and now it was time to return her to her rightful owners. She grabbed the cat carrier and went into the hall with Carnegie, her loyal partner, trotting behind.

Chapter 12

BIJOU

"She got her! Elodie did it!" Oscar's shout was followed by a parkour routine that had him jumping off walls and doing backflips. Elodie was too relieved to have found Bijou to point out the footprints he'd left on the walls.

Tiya was right behind him. "Oh, Bijou! I'm so glad you're back." She held out her arms for Bijou. Whatever ill will Tiya had once had for the cat was long gone. Tiya looked at

Elodie with watery eyes. "How did you know it was Antonio?"

"Because of the article he wrote. I didn't notice it at first, but he included a detail only the catnapper could know."

"No one but us knew Bijou had been taken from Spaw," Oscar said. "We didn't mention it to Ramon, or anyone else, but the Upper West Spy-der included it in the first paragraph."

"Once we realized that, and that the catnapper was looking for publicity, not revenge or money, Antonio was the logical culprit. He was the only one to benefit from Bijou's catnapping and her return."

Tiya looked at Elodie and Oscar awe-struck. "Wow! Only real detectives could have figured all that out."

Any shadows of self-doubt were cast away. Elodie beamed at Tiya's compliment. "Bijou's been found, and Antonio is with the police. Everything worked out, except for one thing," Elodie said and gave Oscar a knowing look as they walked to the elevator. There was one loose end that Elodie was determined to tie up.

The party in the courtyard was in full swing when Elodie and Carnegie returned. No one noticed when Paula slipped out with Phoebe and returned a moment later with Bijou.

Alfie, not quite recovered from the day's ups and downs, sat on a bench mopping his brow. Elodie joined him, noting his linen suit, which had been perfectly pressed when she'd seen him in the lobby, was now rumpled. "I'm not taking any more animals as clients if that's why you're here," he said, looking down at Carnegie.

"It's not," Elodie said and directed Alfie's attention to the doors into The Biltmore. Freddy and Ramon opened them as Oscar unicycled out and flipped into a handstand on the seat. There were plenty of *oohs* and *ahs* from the crowd.

He sat back down and picked up the pace, cycling around the path until he had a clear shot of the fountain. It was the trick he'd been working on since the day he moved into The Biltmore. Would he succeed? If there was ever a moment for him to nail the stunt, this was it.

He had a crowd of actors, including stuntman Lance, and Alfie, an agent, watching.

Pumping his legs, he sped toward the fountain and leapt off the unicycle, somersaulted through the air, and landed on the edge in a perfect dismount. Everyone clapped and cheered. Oscar flung an arm out like he was a Flying Wallenda at a circus finale, beaming at the crowd.

"His name is Oscar Delgado," Elodie told Alfie. "And he is a stuntman, er, stuntboy."

Alfie wasted no time jumping up and going to chat with Oscar. Out of the corner of her eye, Elodie saw that Lance hadn't just been watching, he'd been clapping too. Had Oscar caught him at a bad moment earlier? Or was he really soured toward a career in stunting. Either way, there was no denying Oscar's talent, and now someone who could help him break into the business had seen it.

Elodie, Oscar, and Miss Rosa were tidying up the courtyard. Alfie's business card stuck out of Oscar's pocket. He and his mom had a meeting next week to discuss Oscar's future in the stunting industry. Even better, Lance had come over afterwards to shake Oscar's hand. "Sorry about earlier. I'd just found out I'd lost a gig. This business can wear you down, especially when you've been in it as long as I have." His tough-guy demeanor softened when he looked at Oscar. "But what you did on that unicycle, that was impressive, kid. You've got real talent."

When Lance turned away, Oscar did a backflip of joy.

Tiya was helping Bijou open her gifts as Paula looked on. Despite the ordeal, now that Bijou was back where she belonged, she looked perfectly content. Monsieur Saint Martin had wanted his beloved cat surrounded by luxury. And she was, because real luxury wasn't just about where you lived, but with who.

As the day faded to dusk, Elodie gazed at the now peaceful courtyard. Carnegie yawned, tired after a big day of insniffigating. It was time to head home to #5D. Elodie looked forward to rehashing the day with Miss Rosa and a nice long cuddle with Carnegie. If solving the catnapping case had taught her anything, it was to hold those she loved close.

THE END.

ACKNOWLEDGEMENTS

As always, a huge thank you to the team at Pajama Press: Emma Davis, Quinn Baker, Simin Dewji, Jenny La, and of course, publisher Gail Winskill!

Peggy Collins creates the most magical illustrations to bring these characters to life. It's a dream to work with someone so talented.

The character of Bijou was modeled after Karl Lagerfeld's cat Choupette, who did not inherit his fortune, but who does live in the lap of luxury with her nanny since the fashion designer's death. Her Instagram account @choupetteofficiel provided lots of inspiration for Bijou.

◦❯ **PRAISE FOR** ❮◦

MYSTERY at the BILTMORE #1
The Vanderhoff Heist

"Move over, Eloise at the Plaza: It's Elodie at the Biltmore….Nelson draws out the mystery…providing a satisfying solution….An entertaining blend of quirky characters and locked-room puzzle."

—*Kirkus Reviews*

"An engaging chapter-book mystery….Nelson's characters are funny and well-rounded….Collins' full-color, cartoon illustrations capture each character's quirkiness and reflect the racial diversity of a New York City apartment complex."

—*Booklist*

"This engaging mystery, a series starter for early readers...charms from page one. Elodie is a delightful lead character who demonstrates logic and compassion as she investigates, all the while fighting through doubts that she's too young to be a detective."

—*Publishers Weekly*

"There's a new young detective in New York City, and her name is Elodie LaRue....Overall, this book can find an audience with readers who want to see an independent and assertive main character."

—*School Library Journal*

"Charming. The Biltmore, Elodie, and Oscar (and as always, a cute puppy) make this a total win."

—**Kevin Sylvester, award-winning author of *Apartment 713***

CELEBRATING OUR RECENT AWARDS FOR

THE UMBRELLA HOUSE

★ **2024 TD CANADIAN CHILDREN'S LITERATURE AWARD FINALIST** ★

★ **2023 JUNIOR LIBRARY GUILD SELECTION** ★

★ **2025 NYSRA CHARLOTTE AWARD NOMINEE** ★

★ **2024 FOREST OF READING SILVER BIRCH NOMINEE** ★

★ **2023 INDIGO TOP 50 BEST KIDS' BOOKS OF THE YEAR** ★